ERE BEGINS THE TALE OF THE MARVELLOUS BLUE MOUSE

AUTHORED AND ILLUMINATED BY CHRISTOPHER MANSON

HENRY HOLT + CO. NY

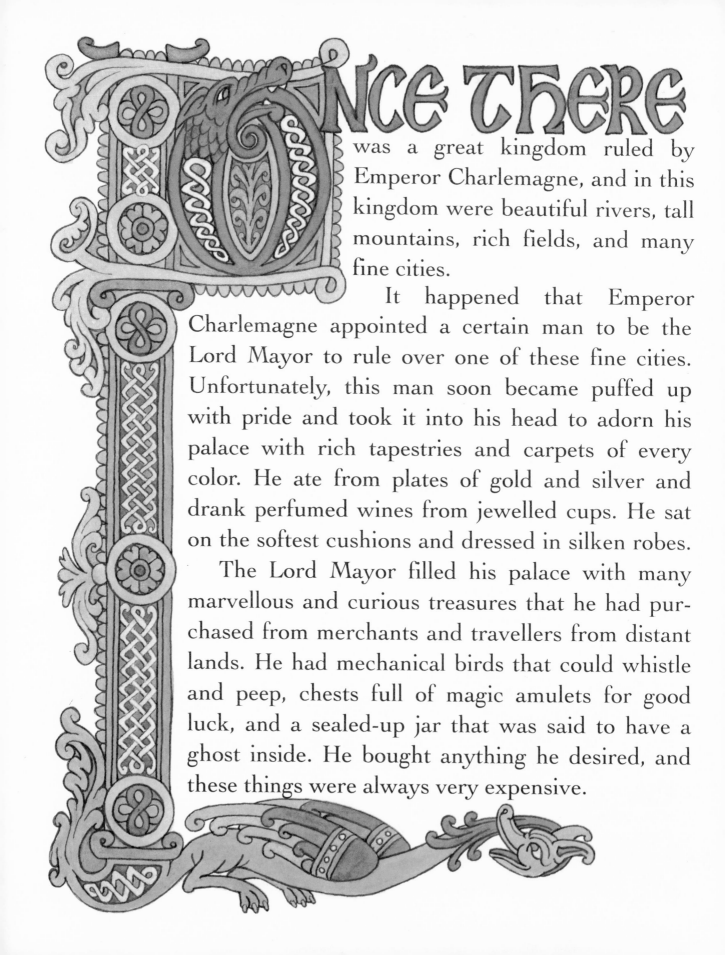

ONCE THERE was a great kingdom ruled by Emperor Charlemagne, and in this kingdom were beautiful rivers, tall mountains, rich fields, and many fine cities.

It happened that Emperor Charlemagne appointed a certain man to be the Lord Mayor to rule over one of these fine cities. Unfortunately, this man soon became puffed up with pride and took it into his head to adorn his palace with rich tapestries and carpets of every color. He ate from plates of gold and silver and drank perfumed wines from jewelled cups. He sat on the softest cushions and dressed in silken robes.

The Lord Mayor filled his palace with many marvellous and curious treasures that he had purchased from merchants and travellers from distant lands. He had mechanical birds that could whistle and peep, chests full of magic amulets for good luck, and a sealed-up jar that was said to have a ghost inside. He bought anything he desired, and these things were always very expensive.

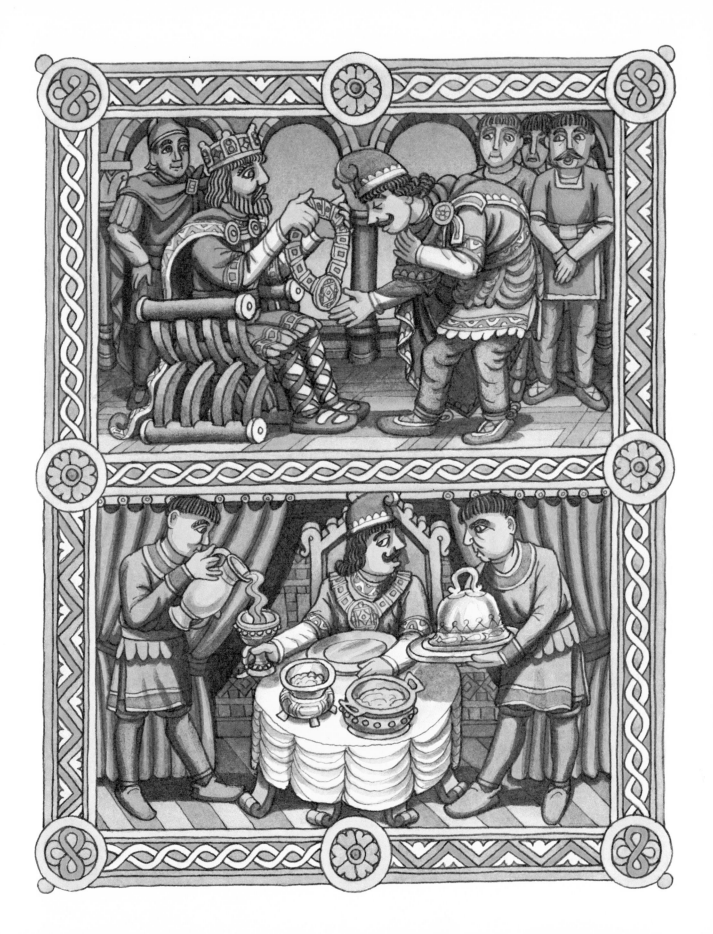

ow the More

of these marvellous things the Lord Mayor owned, the more marvellous he thought he was. Soon enough, he began to feel as important as the Emperor himself, and he never gave a thought to the people of the city.

The city was full of poor people who had no place to live, and almost nothing to eat. Many of the houses and markets were falling down, the streets had holes in them, and even the great walls and towers that protected the city were cracked.

UT THE LORD

Mayor continued to spend the gold in the treasury on himself. Finally, the people came to his rich palace and complained.

The Lord Mayor put his nose up in the air and said, "How dare you complain to me! Emperor Charlemagne himself gave me this city to rule. If you say bad things about me, you are saying bad things about the Emperor."

And at this, the people were afraid to speak out again.

The Emperor

Charlemagne heard rumors of what was happening in the city, and he was vexed beyond measure. "How dare that puffed-up Lord Mayor ruin my beautiful city and impoverish my people, and say that he does this in my name!"

The nobles at Charlemagne's court were quick to suggest many terrible punishments for the Lord Mayor.

"I will take an army of soldiers and attack the city," one said. "And when I capture the scoundrel, I will chop off his head. Then the people will see you are powerful and should be feared."

"I will sail to Africa in a fleet of ships and bring back wild lions and leopards," another said. "I will let them loose in the palace, and the rogue will be torn to pieces. Then the people will see you are as fierce as a lion and as swift as a leopard, and should be feared."

Then Charlemagne's friend Isaac stepped forward. "O Most Noble Emperor!" he said. "It is better that you humble this proud and greedy Lord Mayor, and make the city whole again. Then the people will see that you are merciful as well as just."

Charlemagne liked Isaac's idea. "Will you take armies of soldiers or fleets of ships to humble him?" he asked.

"Neither, Your Majesty," said Isaac with a bow. "I will take only . . . a little mouse!"

ISAAC WENT UP-

stairs and downstairs in the Emperor's palace looking for a mouse. Now, even the grandest palace has a few mice living in it, and it wasn't long before he found just the mouse he wanted. Isaac went to the palace kitchens and took pinches of cinnamon and nutmeg and cloves. Then he made a beautiful little box, and went into his room and closed the door.

When Isaac came out of his room, the beautiful box was painted in lovely colors and the lid was firmly closed. He brought it to the Emperor. With a bow Isaac said, "I am ready, Your Majesty. If you will follow me to the Lord Mayor's city, you will see justice done."

"It shall be as you wish," said Charlemagne.

So Isaac left the Emperor's palace with the beautiful box. After travelling all day, Isaac arrived at the Lord Mayor's city.

HEN ISAAC CAME

near the city he saw that the walls were practically falling down, the great watchtowers had cracked, and the gates were rusty and hardly able to close.

Inside the city . . . well, it was even worse.

There were so many holes in the street, you could hardly walk from here to there.

THE HOUSES HAD

leaky roofs and looked as if they were about to fall down.

And the poor people!

There were so many cold, hungry people begging in the street that Isaac felt ashamed for the Lord Mayor.

BUT THE PALACE

was beautiful. Every room was filled with costly things. Isaac could see that even Emperor Charlemagne himself lived more simply than this Lord Mayor!

The palace was filled with merchants and travellers, all clamoring for the Lord Mayor's attention, and each claiming to have the rarest and most marvellous things to sell.

One said, "Your Lordship, I have a statue from the Land of Egypt that spoke when the sun rose."

Another said, "Your Honor, I have two unicorn horns from the Island of Tin."

Another said, "Your Worship, I have a bag of pearls from the Land of Crim-Tartary. Each pearl controls the destiny of a mighty dragon in a far-off country."

But Isaac stayed back, and said nothing.

The merchants were making so much noise that it was some time before the Lord Mayor looked up and noticed that Isaac was standing there. Then he saw that Isaac was carrying a beautiful little box and holding it very carefully.

"Who is this fellow?" asked the Lord Mayor, pointing at Isaac. "And what does he bring?"

But no one could tell him who Isaac was or what he had brought.

ℭHE LORD MAYOR

put his nose in the air and said, "Come forward, fellow. Who are you and what have you in that little box?"

Isaac stepped forward and waited until there was silence in the great hall. He, too, put his nose up in the air and said, "My Lord Mayor, I have travelled far and wide through many great kingdoms. I have crossed surging seas and burning deserts in search of the rarest, most marvellous thing in all the world."

The Lord Mayor's eyes grew round with wonder.

"And," Isaac said, "I have finally found the rarest and most marvellous thing, in the Kingdom of Babylon!"

THE LORD MAYOR

forgot to keep his nose in the air.

Isaac leaned closer to the Lord Mayor and whispered, "My lord, what these other merchants have brought is as nothing compared to what I possess." And he tapped his little box.

All the merchants shouted, "What an impudent fellow! What can he possibly have in that tiny box to compare with our treasures?" They crowded around Isaac, but he held the box closely to him, so no one could see.

WELL, THE FOOLISH

Lord Mayor was beside himself with curiosity. "My friend!" he said to Isaac. "You have come so far, show me what you have in the box!"

"Yes, yes," said the merchants eagerly. "Show us, show us!"

But Isaac shook his head, saying, "My lord, you must first send these others away—the rarest and most marvellous thing in all the world is not for everyone to see."

The Lord Mayor paused for a minute to think, "This fellow must surely have something very special." So he ordered the merchants to leave the hall right away, and since the Lord Mayor's word was law, they had to go whether they liked it or not.

Isaac ordered that a table be brought into the hall, and it was. Then he ordered that a clean cloth be laid over the table, and it was. Then he ordered that a golden plate be placed right in the center of the cloth, and that was done too.

While the Lord Mayor waited, fidgeting impatiently, Isaac placed the little box right in the center of the golden plate. The Lord Mayor leaned closer. Isaac pushed back his sleeves and carefully lifted the lid of the box. The Lord Mayor leaned over so closely that his nose almost touched the box. A sweet, spicy smell rose in the air.

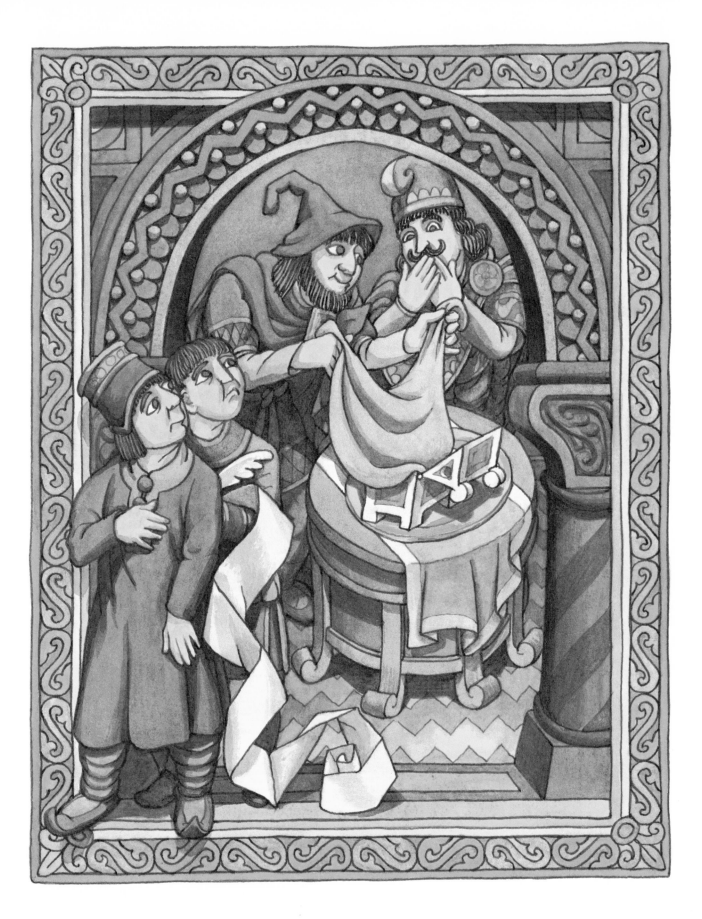

Isaac Unfolded

the colorful silk inside the box. The Lord Mayor couldn't believe his eyes! There, sitting up, was . . . a blue mouse!

His fur was blue, his tail was blue, his feet were blue, his ears were blue. Even his whiskers were blue.

The mouse twitched his whiskers at the Lord Mayor. Then he hopped out of the box and began to nibble on the table-cloth.

"This," said Isaac grandly, "is the rarest and most marvellous thing in the world."

"But it's a mouse!" said the Lord Mayor.

"Not just any mouse," said Isaac. "This is none other than the Marvellous Blue Mouse of Babylon! Notice his wonderful perfume and his incredible blueness. A mouse like this is found only once in a thousand years. . . . King Solomon had one, you know."

"Well!" said the Lord Mayor. "If it is so marvellous, I will give you three pounds of silver for it."

Three pounds of silver was a lot of money, but Isaac pretended to be upset. "A fine price for so marvellous a thing as this!" he cried. "I would take him back to Babylon, first."

"Very well," said the Lord Mayor. "I will give you three pounds of gold for it."

Isaac pretended to be angry. "May I be struck by lightning!" he cried. "I could not accept so little for such a marvellous thing!" And he started to put the mouse back in his box.

NOW EACH TIME

that Isaac refused to accept so much money for the little mouse, the Lord Mayor was more convinced that it was very valuable. After all, who ever heard of someone refusing to sell a little mouse for so much gold?

So the Lord Mayor said, "Wait! I must have the blue mouse for my very own. I will give you twenty pounds of gold for it!"

Isaac pretended to be even angrier and rolled his eyes back and forth and up and down. "I can't bear to hear any more," he said. "Shall all the troubles, pains, and labors I have endured be for nothing? Have I crossed so many oceans and deserts to be cheated of my reward at the end? I will take this mouse to the Emperor, who will surely know its worth!"

The Lord Mayor couldn't bear the thought of someone else owning such a marvel, so at last he offered Isaac all the gold and silver in his palace for the little blue mouse.

"It is not really enough," said Isaac with a sigh. "But I am so worn-out with all your haggling and bargaining that I will accept. The Marvellous Blue Mouse of Babylon is yours."

It Took a Long

time for Isaac to count up the enormous pile of treasure. All the money that should have been spent to keep the city safe and clean and strong was in that pile.

And while Isaac was counting, the Lord Mayor was gazing fondly at the blue mouse, who had nibbled a hole in the table-cloth. The Lord Mayor was so taken with his new possession that he failed to notice the arrival of Emperor Charlemagne.

"Ahem!" said the Emperor.

"Your Ma-ma-majesty!" stammered the Lord Mayor. "I had no idea that you were coming to visit!"

I CAN SEE THAT,

said the Emperor sternly. "What have you done to my beautiful city?"

The Lord Mayor drew himself up with his nose in the air. "I have enriched it, Your Majesty. You see, I have collected the rarest and most marvellous things in all the world. People everywhere speak of the wonders to be found in this city."

"I have seen some of those wonders on my way to your palace," said Charlemagne sadly. "It is a wonder that the city walls are still standing! It is a wonder that anyone can find a way through the streets full of holes and trash! It is a wonder that the people can find anything to eat at all!"

ELL, REALLY, YOUR

Majesty," said the Lord Mayor, "everything looks fine from the windows of my palace. I look outside at least once every day to be sure. And now, let me show you some of the marvels I have collected to glorify your realm."

"What is this dusty old chair?" asked Charlemagne.

The Lord Mayor answered, "That chair once belonged to Alexander the Great himself."

"How do you know that?" asked Charlemagne.

The Lord Mayor pointed to the seat and said, "You can see where he carved his initials there: A.G."

"What is this tin trumpet?" asked Charlemagne.

The Lord Mayor

said, "If you put it to your ear on the night of the full moon, you can hear the moon people talking."

"What do they say?" asked Charlemagne.

The Lord Mayor shrugged his shoulders. "Well, so far they have been very quiet."

"And what is this little mouse?" asked Charlemagne.

"This—" said the Lord Mayor proudly, "this is the rarest and most wonderful thing in all the world! May I present to Your Majesty the Marvellous Blue Mouse of Babylon. . . ."

Charlemagne smiled and turned to Isaac. "What do you think of this, my friend?" he said.

Isaac Looked

at the little mouse, who was trying to nibble on a piece of gold, and he looked at the great heap of treasure the Lord Mayor had paid for it.

"O Most Noble Emperor!" said Isaac with a bow. "I cannot speak for any of these other things, but this is, truly, a most wonderful mouse. He can show us how wise, how just, and how prudent this Lord Mayor is."

"How can a little mouse do all this?" asked Charlemagne.

"I need only a bowl of water," said Isaac, and a bowl of water was brought to him.

Then, before the eyes of the Lord Mayor, the Emperor, and the entire Imperial court, Isaac picked up the Marvellous Blue Mouse by the tail and . . . dipped him in the water.

The little mouse splashed around in the water for a minute, and when Isaac took him out of the bowl, the water was bright blue and the mouse was gray!

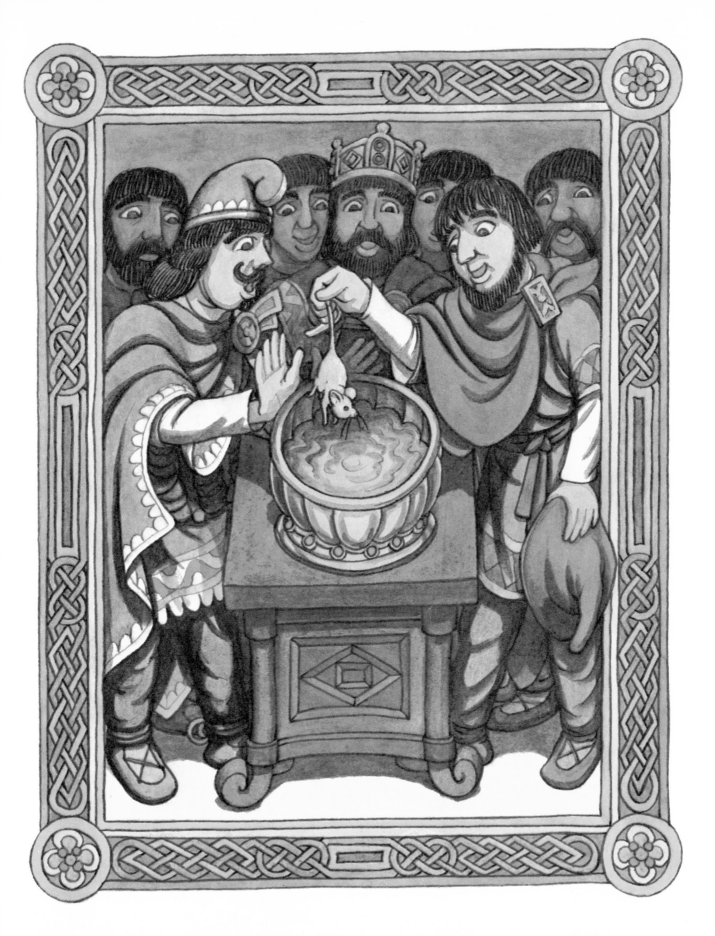

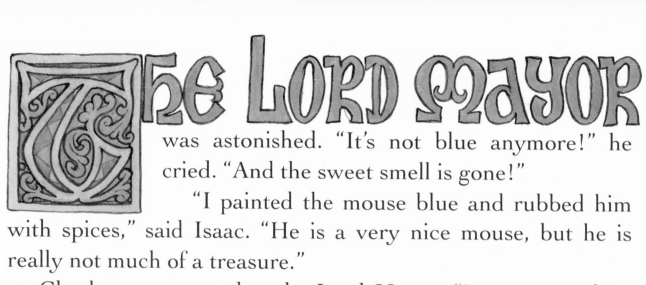

THE LORD MAYOR

was astonished. "It's not blue anymore!" he cried. "And the sweet smell is gone!"

"I painted the mouse blue and rubbed him with spices," said Isaac. "He is a very nice mouse, but he is really not much of a treasure."

Charlemagne turned to the Lord Mayor. "It was your duty to keep my city safe, to look after my people, to minister to the poor," he roared. "Instead, you have given all this treasure for a painted and perfumed mouse. Everyone shall hear the tale of your foolishness, and you shall be banished from my realm forever. Be gone!"

And the Lord Mayor had his chain of office taken away. Then he was taken away.

The Emperor had all the Lord Mayor's treasure given back to the people so that the city could be made safe and strong and clean again. Then Charlemagne said, "Now who will rule this city for me?

PERHAPS I WILL

let this truly marvellous mouse choose the new Lord Mayor—he seems to be a better judge of character than I."

Just then, the mouse hopped into Isaac's hand. "He has chosen you, Isaac," said Charlemagne. "And so it shall be."

And that is how Isaac became Lord Mayor of a great city, which he ruled wisely and well for many years.

Author's Note

The story of the blue mouse was written down in the year A.D. 884 by a monk called Notker the Stammerer. I have changed a few details, but the Emperor, Isaac, and the mouse were all there to expose the folly and greed of an important man for everyone to see. Part of the trick was the use of spices to give the mouse a special fragrance, and back then spices from Asia were much rarer and more expensive than they are today. The little mouse must have truly seemed to have something of the marvellous about him.

◆

This book is for young Matthew F., of course. —*C.M.*

◆

Published by Henry Holt and Company, Inc., 115 West 18th Street, New York, New York 10011.
Published simultaneously in Canada by Fitzhenry & Whiteside Ltd., 195 Allstate Parkway, Markham, Ontario L3R 4T8.

Library of Congress Cataloging-in-Publication Data
Manson, Christopher. The Marvellous Blue Mouse / written and illustrated by Christopher Manson. Summary: A trusted adviser to Emperor Charlemagne uses a small mouse and some ingenuity to expose the misdeeds of a greedy Lord Mayor. ISBN 0-8050-1622-8 1. Charlemagne, Emperor, 742–814—Juvenile Fiction. [1. Charlemagne, Emperor, 742–814—Fiction. 2. Greed—Fiction. 3. Mice—Fiction.] I. Title PZ7.M31825Mar 1992 [E]—dc20 91-29131

Henry Holt books are available at special discounts for bulk purchases for sales promotions, premiums, fund-raising, or educational use. Special editions or book excerpts can also be created to specification.
First edition   Printed in the United States of America on acid-free paper. ∞
1 3 5 7 9 10 8 6 4 2